THE SEVEN JEWEL BIRD

fiction

by

ROBERT STIKMANZ

STIKMANTICA

AUSTIN & MONTEVIDEO

Cover illustration, book design and entire contents by Robert Stikmanz

1501024

ISBN   978-1-7321187-4-4

Cataloging Data
The Seven Jewel Bird / Robert Stikmanz
         p.   cm.
         ISBN 978-1-7321187-4-4
         I. Stikmanz, Robert
              1. Fiction—Slipstream—Future

stikmantica.com

THE SEVEN JEWEL BIRD

The weathered tiles were brittle; one broke under the weight as the old man wrestled his cart forward. The cart slewed, hit the entry wall, and locked in place, one wheel jammed in a new divot. The man yanked it backward, shoved through the entry, and stopped.

The space in which he stood rose eleven stories. Set into the front of the building, it had once been a lobby, but the glass that had closed its face was long gone. Pausing to swipe a bandana over his neck and forehead, the man scanned the building before moving closer.

Three cars sat near the foot of the stairs. Two were human-powered, but one had a four-cylinder combustion engine. Movement on the fifth floor landing he ignored. The rare shadows that came and went from that level never welcomed scrutiny. On the first landing, his own, a young woman in a trisuit stretched. Looking up, she grinned.

"Maker!" she called. "Hey!"

He flushed, and half waved.

Then he remembered to smile, though the smile was more a softening around his eyes than a change of expression. The woman winked at him as she pushed further into her stretch. He noted the visual composition, her green and blue garment vivid against the rust-colored wall between their doors.

"Carlotta," he muttered.

Her name was Carlotta. Saying it aloud confirmed it.

She read his lips and grinned wider.

Maker shoved the cart forward. At the foot of the stairs, he swung it around and backed to the first step.

"Hey!" Carlotta objected. "You'll hurt yourself."

Laughing, she hurried down and eased around him, grabbing the front of the cart.

"Ready?" she asked.

This time when he smiled, his mouth actually twitched.

She took the weight step by step as they climbed, lifting as he pulled. Though slight, she was strong, and alternately crouched and stood to raise the load. Maker, struggling to haul up his end of the bargain, was fascinated by her grace. She caught him looking, which earned another grin.

Her affection always puzzled him.

The cart was filled with gleaningS from the market under the ex-freeway. He was grateful for her help, but it also made him shy. His thanks at the top of the stairs were mumbled. Carlotta answered over her shoulder, already reaching for her door.

"Are you ready?" she cooed as she pushed it open.

A miniature greyhound trotted out, leash in mouth.

"Peppy," Maker mouthed silently. Her dog's name was Peppy.

It sniffed toward him and wagged as Carlotta snapped the leash to its collar. Thoughts shifting elsewhere, Maker watched them descend the stairs.

When the superintendant had introduced the couple, Maker almost overlooked her. Well-meaning but uncertain, he thought. As he was about to dismiss her, she shifted, and he glimpsed the person behind the mask. He saw her register that she had been seen. Really seen.

Bear, her partner, registered it, too. Inhaling noisily, the younger man draped an arm across her shoulders.

By Maker's guess, Bear was wound half a turn too tight. He wore it like a habit.

"We're living together on a trial basis," Carlotta volunteered. "Bear asked me to marry him, but I said we should try a year first, and then see if we want to make it permanent."

Bear smiled possessively, pulling her against his side.

"I never thought about it," he admitted, "but she's right. There's more than having the right architecture. It's always give and take, but I like what I like. Besides," he gave her a squeeze and a shake, "If she makes the year, I'll pay off her loans as a wedding present. That's real incentive."

Carlotta flushed, and looked away.

On impulse, Maker excused himself. He returned immediately, winding the spring on a mechanical brass tea rose.

Handing it to her, he said, "A gift at the start of your adventure."

She pressed the release and the tight bud bloomed. Even Bear was impressed. He took it from her and held it up, captivated by the dull gleam of the petals.

"I'd normally take a dim view of another man giving my woman flowers," he told them, "But that's pretty cool."

Handing it back to Carlotta, he ordered, "Now take it inside while I talk business with the old man."

Her eyes flashed, but she said nothing. Bear pointedly watched her walk away. After she disappeared through the door, he turned to Maker.

"Supe here says you're the man to connect our juice. How fast can we get that done?"

Maker considered.

"This afternoon. I can make time after Mr. Idris's son gets home."

He turned to the superintendent.

"Kam gets back around three, right?"

"Now is better," Bear objected.

"No."

Maker shook his head.

"Impossible. It means a trip to the roof,

and I don't go higher than the third floor without an escort."

He indicated the superintendent.

"That's Mr. Idris, his son, and their pump-action shotguns. I think Kam gets back around three."

"What the hell?"

Bear looked from one to the other.

"Who's up there?"

Eyebrows high, Maker gazed expectantly at Mr. Idris. Mr. Idris gazed at nothing as he considered his answer.

At last, he said, "Not everyone pays rent in what passes for currency. Like him."

He jutted his chin toward Maker.

"But some of them really don't like to be disturbed."

He shrugged.

"And some of them have, ah...."

He cleared his throat.

"Pets."

He shrugged again.

"Life in this sector. You're the ones who came slumming."

"What the hell," Bear repeated, this time a statement. "I can handle a pump. Let's do this."

Maker sighed, inclining his head in deference to the man with the guns.

"Mr. Idris?"

The superintendent conceded, raising his palms.

"Now? Okay, sure. Let me get the sisters."

   After that first day, Maker was ever standoffish. Carlotta stubbornly liked him anyway. So did Peppy. Bear pretended he was beneath notice.

Increasingly, strain marked Carlotta. She
often looked half weary and half wary.
When the tension dropped away, like when
helping Maker on the stairs, she was radiant.

Once, rushing out the door, he stumbled into her warm-up. She threw out an arm to stop him from pitching forward. Laughing, she steadied him. He reached toward her smile without thinking. She raised her face to brush his finger with her cheek.

Automatically cataloging the sensation, he murmured, "Velvet satin. Satin velvet? Satin velvet."

Another day she gave him a business card showing M.Sc. after her name and a title, Clinical Nutritionist. The logo and contact information were for a consumer health agency.

"I mostly oversee pre-K breakfast programs," she told him. "It's all ordering and distributing manufactured meals, which is ironic. I would rather teach people to cook."

Her expression clouded, giving way for an instant to the mask. She put it off, and shrugged.

"I'm thinking about medical school."

Maker nodded, taking it in.

"Your partner," he asked, "What does he do?"

Carlotta shook her head.

"When I asked, all he said was that it's legal and profitable. Sometimes he travels."

Large and handsome, Bear was an ex-jock who still worked out, but not as much or as hard as once. He was aggressive, impulsive, quick to anger and demanding. When forced to acknowledge his neighbor, he called him, "old man," or "Mr. Fix-it."

The diesel coupé he drove had window stickers for access to the private road system and an exemption from the combustion tax. His snapping criticism came through the wall every night during the couple's supper.

Although densely used, the front room of Maker's space was well ordered. A clock on the wall tocked to its pendulum. Beneath a glass dome, a smaller, pedestal clock ticked almost but not quite in sync. Otherwise, the place was usually quiet.

Counters, work benches, and the recliner he used for a bed left a maze of pathways as the only open floor. Objects in various stages of manufacture or repair shared space on most of the flat surfaces with broken things scavenged from the market.

Glowing in the diffuse light, mechanical brass flowers escaped the ordered ranks of their precisely filled shelves, clustering here and there like seeding clusters.

A ballerina waited, frozen *en pointe* alongside a windup bear poised to juggle. Inside a glass case, a blue-turbaned fortuneteller, three-quarters life-sized and intricately constructed, if only from the waist up, waited with a deck of cards for an extinct coin to set it in motion.

Around works in progress, there were tools and parts and the press of brass flowers, but no clutter. The flowers rose in dozens and threes, bringing a sense of balance in complexity, a rightness, to the room.

The counter where the flowers were made was most organized of all. With two pairs of pliers, a half dozen clips, and sorted supplies of each different piece, he could produce any one of seven designs, from memory, at a rate of three an hour. His proficiency meant he spent several days a month casting and milling the pieces of a windup garden. Every trip to the market under the old freeway included hunting and haggling for scraps of brass.

Each flower stood, he would attest, "25 centimeters, give or take," on a recurved stem that flared into a pedestal at the bottom. Winding the stem closed the bloom into a bud. Releasing a catch caused the bloom to open. At once toy and sculpture, the devices were of no practical use. They were wildly popular, especially if Maker provided a certificate.

More than a fallback, the profusion of flowers was part of his legend. His designs were copied — they were elegantly simple — but only those bearing his mark were perfect. Other crafters were skilled, but even those who copied faithfully admitted that the old man never just made or repaired anything. He was called a wizard, and some really believed it.

One spot in the room was free of flowers. A table pulled out from the wall he shared with Bear and Carlotta stood raised on blocks. The floor around it was clear for access on all sides. At its center, a mechanical bird stared from a perch rising out of an incomplete assembly of rods and gears. It seemed a creature born to flit through gardens of brass.

Finch-like, it was made so that the bright wings would spread and flutter, and the head turn, lifting its face. The mouth was articulated to open and close, and the tail made to fan while shifting up and down. Its parts were enameled, the chest in turquoise, the head and back, including the backs of the wings and tail, in lapis lazuli. Gleaming scarlet tipped the flight feathers.

Maker closed his door, turned toward the bird, and was arrested by the sight. His hands twitched, remembering its construction. What he saw as he stared was both the state it had reached and what it would become.

This was the machine that pushed his limits. The wonder-worker reputation was useful in business, but Maker had never worn it lightly. The weight would be unbearable if no truth backed it. With this bird he was taking his own measure.

He scrutinized it lovingly. Anxiously.

Finally, having looked enough, he crossed the room.

In a corner still identifiable as a kitchenette, he spread bean paste on a rice cake and took one large bite before setting it aside. He punched the start sequence on his electroplator as he chewed. Leftover tea washed down the mouthful. He filled the unrinsed cup with hot, ersatz coffee, which he forgot completely as soon as the interface on the electroplator's screen stabilized with a blink. His bird still had no voice. That mattered more than breakfast.

Actually, the bird had sung, but only with placeholder scales.

At the heart of the mechanism were two spiny cylinders modified from old music boxes. Placing them precisely called for testing, and that required something for the spines to hit. The temporary scales he used were lovely, but polymer tines were not capable of clear, shattering tones. The music demanded an engine as wondrous as itself.

The cylinders were not originals, but adapted versions. The model for one had played a tune by Mozart; the other, a melody of Poulenc. Maker scanned the cylinders, but before printing he shifted a few spines on each to positions more visually elegant. He also resized the new versions so they would turn at a matched rate.

As in a music box, his bird sang when spines on the rotating cylinders struck tines arranged in flat combs. A typical music box has one set of tines. The bird had three.

Arranged in a merry-go-round of offset gears, the cylinders revolved as well as rotated. Maker devised a one-beat, skip-shift randomizer so the cylinders would shift with deliberate irregularity.

Phrases no longer either Mozart or Poulenc traded off in a splice with chance.

At some point — given a finite number of variables — Maker knew the action of the assembly would repeat. Eventually, tines and cylinders would return to initial positions. Given enough of these returns, even jumped by the shift, some slice of possible combinations would duplicate. Early in the building process he had started to calculate a likely timeframe for this to happen. The question grew urgent when he realized that in a scenario of infinite play repetition was inevitable. Once he determined that likelihood was small he would live to hear it, his curiosity turned elsewhere.

Slipping on white cotton gloves before opening the electroplator, Maker removed his chosen scales. These had not come from the music boxes that inspired the cylinders, but from others more ancient and remote.

"Broken relics" from a ruined tower that once guarded a lost empire. At least, so claimed his friend, Doña Laura de las Casas, the vendor in the market who had sold them.

"Trebizondo," she had said. "An ancient land on a hidden sea, that thrived on secret trade."

Maker had no reason to disbelieve her.

Whatever their source, they were very old, and built on strange intervals that, to him, seemed otherworldly. Tarnish had dulled their sound and corrupted the notes, but Maker cleaned them with a conservator's skill, and analyzed their frequencies. The electroplator laid down an outer skin of gold atom by atom. If he had figured it right, the original tones were restored and perfected.

Carefully, willing his hands not to shake, he affixed the combs to mounts on the resonator. He plucked each tine with a toothpick. Crystalline, enormous, the tones rang out and slowly faded.

The sound lanced through him, excruciating in a way beyond words.

Pressure built in his chest with the slow, chiming steps of the scales, driving his heart wild. The world shivered.

Astonished, Maker fiddled with the toothpick. He labored to control his breathing.

Steadiness came back reluctantly. When he could trust his grip again, he tightened tiny screws to adjust the cylinders, then let his hands fall to his sides. The ticking and tocking of the clocks seemed to grow louder. The bird perched atop its machinery.

Maker caressed the frame on which the cylinders were mounted. Pushing the assembly slowly through its cycle, he heard halting notes play as a sequence. A melody began to emerge, an air with phrasing not Mozart, not Poulenc. Sudden tears started from his eyes. He retreated to the bathroom to splash water on his face.

He stretched, trying to dismiss the rush of emotion. Tears hovered stubbornly close. The feeling was too real to discount as imaginary, and unaccountable if not provoked by those sounds.

But how?

Generally, he kept emotion of any sort well bottled.

A rumble from his gut brought him back

to the mundane. He finished breakfast while staring at the bird, washing down the rice cake and bean paste with room temperature ersatz. In the aftermath of that penetrating sequence, the mismatched tempos of the two clocks were reassuringly ordinary.

It bothered him that the inexplicable sadness did not fade. He hesitated to try another test. Reluctantly setting aside the empty cup, he slipped the gloves back on.

Gingerly, with a fingertip, he pushed the machine through a cycle.

The two cylinders rotated and revolved, changing scales as they changed combs. The combs moved back and forth to vary the notes hit by the spines. Occasionally, the skip-one randomizer shifted a cylinder, and the music paused for a beat. The periods of the subassemblies differed, eliminating any simple pattern. Even this slow, halting succession evolved constantly.

Maker had yet to design a way to automate the bird, so he fashioned a temporary crank tied to the gear train. With one deep breath, in and out, he started rotating the handle. To hear was to learn.

The enclosure for the mechanical works was a resonating chamber that amplified the sound. When he fit it into place and turned

the crank the music boomed. He had
provided for volume control with a lever
that lowered a plush-lined cap around the
base. He set it almost closed, but realized he
was not ready for more. Instead, he turned
away and began to bustle around the room,
collecting his wits and inventory for another
trip to the market.

He filled a box snugly with brass flowers,
considered the swaths remaining, and filled
another.

That night, after heavy drinking with friends in their living room, Bear beat Carlotta. Maker heard everything. He knew what was happening as if he stood in their room. At the first smack, he flashed on the black eye she would wear the next day.

Maker dithered. He went onto the landing and crossed to their door, but stopped before knocking. Leaning with a hand against its veneer, he listened as Bear shouted and punched. Carlotta begged to know what he is doing. She implored him to stop. Maker slammed his own door when he shut himself in.

Through the wall, he heard Bear accuse, "I saw you roll your eyes when I was talking! I saw you do it! You goddamned don't disrespect me like that!"

He struck her again, and again. In desperation, Maker seized the crank on the bird and ground frantically. He pushed the volume fully open. When Bear heard, Maker thought, he would realize that he, too, was heard.

Exquisite notes burst into the room, shattering against the walls. Through his feet, Maker felt the floor shudder in resonance. The blows stopped. Maker kept cranking.

After a moment, almost lost in the song, sounds came from the other apartment. A door closed. Water ran. Another door closed loudly. A door opened, then the apartment door, then Carlotta's steps hurried across the landing and half ran down the stairs.

Somehow, through a gale of melody, Maker heard this. Though he continued to crank, he heard the dog whine.

The next afternoon, Bear was waiting when Carlotta returned. He sat on the top stair, blocking the landing. Her dog strained in his arms. Maker had started out earlier, seen Bear in place, and changed his mind. From behind his door, he heard Bear shout at Carlotta's ride to be careful of his car.

To Carlotta, Bear said, "Peppy couldn't figure out where you were. Come inside."

The landing creaked as the couple retreated to their apartment.

Hardly muffled, Bear's words came through the wall.

"You know how to push my buttons, and you should know not to do that. I love you, but I can't be responsible if you provoke me. Everything is fine when you don't do that."

The woman said something Maker could not make out.

"Don't tell me you weren't provoking me!" Bear snapped. "Don't say it! Just go in the bedroom. I'll be there in a minute."

A moment later Maker heard a door close. Their bedroom was on the side of the apartment away from him. The floor plans were mirrors. He heard Peppy whimper and knew it was in the short hall to the bedroom and bath. Then he heard only ticking clocks.

He exhaled, suddenly aware that he had held his breath. The quiet from the other side of the wall made him uneasy. Trying to shut it out, he made an effort to remember the pattern of his breathing. It was lost. Maker busied himself with a dental pick, scraping at the rockers that shifted the scale combs.

It bothered him that he could not objectify the song. He had a sentimental attachment to all the products of his skill, but the actual material things were almost an afterthought. They were, in a way, fortunate side effects that he could sell or trade. But this hybrid of chance and lilt, this bird, these scrambled phrases and exotic tones, rang with such power that his heart started to pound when he reached for the crank.

Unlike anything else he had ever made, the plan for the musical works had come to him in a flash. He had been inspired before, but never with such instant completeness. There had been no preliminary sketches, no scraps of arithmetic. When he first held the original, tarnished cylinders, a schematic had unfolded in his mind. Instead of a device for repeating a tune, he saw — in all its detail — a fount of ever changing melody.

Examining those reclaimed cylinders of Mozart and Poulenc, he had suddenly wanted to shift a number of spines on each very slightly. Wanted it so imperatively that he had spent an afternoon scanning, altering and printing new versions.

He already knew how the cylinders would fit in an apparatus not yet real. The angle of the scales, the rockers on which they would mount, the hardwood shell for damping the sound, all of it was so clear in his mind that he could put a ruler to empty air for the dimensions. Time evaporated when he set to work.

The bird itself had taken shape days previous. Without even a guiding vision, Maker had switched abruptly from flowers to this new thing. There was no forethought or premonition. He simply put aside a finished rose and began shaping and fitting pieces, some of steel but mostly of brass. Repeatedly surprised, he recognized the aptness of each improvised, half-intuited part as it snugged into place. Once done, he hardly contemplated the exquisite whole before taking it apart to enamel with sure abandon.

All the movements built into the bird grew from the lessons of his flowers. Simple actions combined to mimic the complex motions of avian life. Even now, days later, he felt the small, articulated sculpture was more discovery than the fruit of his hand. The way it rose and bobbed as he cranked, opening and closing its wings, turning this way and that, seemed magical. Its voice could not be less.

Listening for the twentieth time or more,

the volume almost completely closed, he had grown familiar enough with the music's effect that he could, if not suppress it, at least hold it at arm's length. With less passionate ears, he heard two notes stick out. Two notes beautiful in an ordinary way, but no more than that. Having heard, he could not unhear. Every lesser pitch was like a hiccup in the flow.

Maker opened the base and located the problem tines. Using a tiny file as a bow, he adjusted the tuning by ear. Each note swelled as it was corrected. The changes registered palpably. His gut churned as the frequencies closed on ideal, relaxing instantly when the sound was exactly right.

He closed the base and lowered its cap for minimum volume. Maker began to crank, at first listening analytically. But the music drew him in. His movements grew trancelike.

Lulled by the motion, his thoughts slowed and eventually stopped. Even the deepmost babbler in the back of his mind at last fell quiet. Hand and ear linked wordlessly. Unaware he did so, Maker hummed fundamentals of the notes that struck one after another.

He cranked far longer than any need to

test the mechanism or the tines or the bobbing flutter of the bird itself. Suggestive, allusive, the music enveloped him. His shift and sway became a dance.

Daydream, something he had long neglected, slipped free when he ceased to think. In reverie, he soared on the strains that lifted him.

Maker swooped above mountain and forest. A golden streak, he plunged into the sea. Bursting from the deep, he dove, then breached again to skip over cresting waves. He roared onto land. He fought beasts and brigands. Laughing, he tasted dew in his sweat. He wept.

And he loved.

It came back to him.

Once, even he had loved.

Maker had forgotten.

As suddenly as the vision came, it drained away.

Grief made his arm heavy. Clumsy words and, worse, clumsy silences, returned like accusations from the past.

Once, long ago, even he had loved. He had done it badly.

There had been other hopes, and other chances he had missed. And countless disappointments where there had been no chance.

Times, too many times, he had been called to action and failed to act.

Larger than any of those, there had been this once. This one he had loved. Whom he had not loved well enough. She had gone.

There was only himself to blame.

He had done that until he grew weary. Then it had slipped from mind.

Gradually, unnoticed though his hand still held it, Maker stopped turning the handle.

He made things. That had been his rationalization. Without hesitation, he took on any object ever asked of him. Solar arrays, prosthetic limbs, mechanical flowers — by this point hundreds and hundreds of flowers — he made, modified or fixed them all. His repairs spanned the patched-together gamut of tech from before the collapse. Nothing changed the fact that when another heart called for his willing hand, he had kept still.

On the heels of that memory, every choice he had ever avoided streamed back from oblivion. The averted eyes of a life. Remembrance swept through him jabbing an accusing finger at the night just past.

His pulse hammered.

The night just past he had stood in this

room listening to fist strike flesh in the next apartment. The night just past he had done nothing.

His wallow in guilt ended at the sound of a smack and thud against the wall.

Bear was beating Carlotta. Startled, Maker realized it had been happening for some minutes. He had been oblivious. Carlotta's voice was neither crying nor loud. Indistinct, pleading, it came punctuated by blows.

Maker let go of the crank as though burned. Overwhelmed by self-disgust, he began to pace, counting steps loudly to keep thoughts and memory at bay. He kept losing count and starting over. He paced until exhausted, upon which he staggered to his recliner and fell atop the afghan, asleep before he landed.

A pre-dawn summons from a taco wagon took him early to the market. Maker traded repair on a gas griddle for breakfast. He came home to find Carlotta on the landing, in her tri suit, stretching out. The left side of her face was a bruise. Her eye was black and the corner of her mouth was split. She gazed levelly at Maker as he came up the stairs.

Never pausing, she greeted him quietly, "Hello. How are you?"

He could not look away, but he struggled to meet her eye.

At last he replied, "Fine. How are you?"

Their door flew open. Bear stood with a hand on the knob, chest heaving.

"What are you doing, old man?" he snarled.

Maker's pulse raced. He fought to remain steady.

"Just coming home," he answered.

His voice quavered.

Bear puffed his chest, pointedly opening and closing the fist of his free hand.

Maker was afraid. He slunk past Carlotta and shut himself inside his apartment.

The weight of all his days collapsed on him.

He sagged against the door. In the pit of his stomach, his breakfast soured.

Maker looked at the bird. Fear bitter in his mouth, the thought of its song was intolerable. Grabbing a square of microfiber and a swab, he fell upon it, cleaning furiously. Long after even imaginary dust was removed, he scrubbed and buffed.

Sudden queasiness drove him to the bathroom.

He wondered if time had come to change his diet, or his residence, but then his body claimed all his attention.

Avoiding the neighbors, Maker made a point of returning home during the hour when Bear demanded supper. After a few days without meeting either of them, his guard dropped. His inner life, filled with an ongoing, semi-conscious elaboration of the bird, blunted his wariness.

One evening, mentally organizing the tasks that waited, Maker started up the stairs before realizing Bear and a friend slouched in the door of the other apartment.

Their smiles, at first, barely covered their mouths. A hard glimmer flared in the eyes of one, then the other. The smiles grew genuine and terrifying.

Watching his neighbor, Bear drawled, "You have to be careful around here, Rufer. This old man's always listening."

"Really?"

Bear's friend gestured with an open beer. "I think that would annoy me."

Maker fumbled the key into his lock.

Darting inside, he slammed the door and fell against it. His chest heaved around a pounding heart.

Through the wall he heard, "Lotta! Get in here!"

An exchange between the men came through as a slurred murmur.

Bear shouted again, "I said get in here!"

The old man began to shiver. He staggered, pierced by the ice in that voice.

"Heh-heh," Bear laughed. "Come here, baby."

Maker pounced on the bird, cranking frantically with one hand as he shoved the volume lever, trying to force it beyond its limit. Melody exploded into the room. All sound from the other apartment stopped.

Maker would not have known otherwise. He heard nothing but the bird. Its song rang out, bittersweet, a consonance of semi-tones that rode — and shaped — the fever that drove him.

Notes poured forth. Sadness and old magic haunted surging scales from a fallen land.

Yearning struck him hard. His knees threatened to buckle. He kept on.

Later he would remember Bear's voice through the wall.

"Is he crying? What the hell? Is the old guy crying?"

Later, he would remember, but as the bird sang, the world had no other sound.

Maker cranked, rushing the machine to force notes through the wall. The music, always the same unfolding melody, never the same, never quite repeating, called to everything he had let slip away. Unchecked by exertion or fed by it, his loss grew. The ache was palpable. It swelled with failures suppressed

"It was survival!" he raged.

Memory proved stronger than his power to deny. It was not that his transgressions had been large. It was their sheer number.

"Bastard! Bastard!" his heart beat with the song.

Maker sobbed as he cranked.

Of use to no one.

A remnant, a leftover. Dreg of another time. Of no use.

No use, certainly, to the woman beyond the wall.

No use to himself. A blot.

He howled.

Each turn of the handle dredged more darkness.

A way of life, a world of nations had fallen. In the descent, hurt was a currency in which he had dealt. The blackest trades bubbled from forgetfulness, both the gain he had taken and whom it had cost. Never in balance, self-pity was mocked by his own complicit acts. Sometimes irredeemably selfish. Never once had he been brave.

The more the bird sang, the more he relived what he could not endure admitting. With every note, his misery grew.

Miserable or not, he was pulled by the song. Within the anguish beat a promise fulfilled as it was made. Little by little, guilt leached away.

At last, with a hiccup and a belch, he stopped. Maker released the handle and sank to the floor. Momentum drove the bird a little longer. A last few notes staggered into silence.

He blinked and blinked again. Exhausted, he sprawled on the worn carpet and closed his eyes. His heartbeat slowed. His breathing grew steady and deep. Except for the low tock and faster ticking, the room was still.

Maker straightened his legs and smacked his lips. A minute more, and solemn if not sober ears on the other side of the wall clearly heard rumbling snores.

He navigated the market, calling to acquaintances and waving. Everyone knew the old man who made miracles from broken things, at least by sight. Maker knew many of them back. He paid well or traded fairly for mechanical clocks and watches, but anything with gears or pivots attracted his interest. Old tools of any kind were worth bringing to his attention, for raw material as often as for what they were designed to do.

Many vendors knew him, too, as a master of repair. Always alert, always helpful, ever reserved, his grasp of the infrastructure on which so much was built seemed uncanny. Given time and materials, he could fix almost anything. In the heat of a crisis, his patches held. There was not a booth beneath the decaying, decommissioned freeway unknown to him. The market, though it glowed and hummed from numberless small contrivances, owed no small thanks to the old bricoleur.

At a stall filled with cotton goods and stacks of derbies, he tweaked a prosthesis for an injured child. Ten minutes later, the taco seller by the entrance pressed lunch on him after he cleared the gas line to her grill. In the aisle of gleaners who mined the depopulated suburbs, he bargained market scrip for a bucket filled with clipped ends of brass tubing, and traded two mechanical flowers for a garage door spring. He lit incense at the booth shrine of Guanyin and a candle across the aisle for Our Lady.

Buoyant, he steered the cart with grafted-on bicycle wheels effortlessly. A bounce in his step attracted notice.

"Maker!" sounded up the aisles and down the cut-throughs. "Looking good!"

He paused to stretch, relishing limberness he had thought gone forever.

Rolling to a stop beside a booth at the market's heart, he touched a finger to the brim of an imaginary hat. Doña Laura de las Casas, alone beneath the ex-freeway she remembered being built, could appreciate both the irony of the gesture and the genuine respect with which it was meant. The centenarian rose stiffly, waving him close. Taking his hand in both her own, she drew him into the booth.

Her companion, a young girl, jumped to surrender her chair. Maker lowered himself into the seat.

The girl took a spot beside him, her hand on his shoulder. She had come to live with, work for and be schooled by Doña Laura about two years earlier. A lesson she had learned well was that, solemn face or no, Maker was fond of her. When he turned to thank her, she lit up, happy at his attention. For a flash, Carlotta's bruised face hid the girl. Maker's peace drained away.

Dumbstruck, he fell back against the chair. Looking in surprise at Doña Laura, he burst out sobbing.

The vendor swept scrip and a few tokens from her till and handed them to the girl.

"Libertad," she instructed, "Take this to Doña Eva and ask for a canister for the stove. You may stay to have *una horchata.*"

"*Bisabuelita,* I didn't do anything!" Libertad swore, her own eyes tearing. "I promise!"

"*Querida,* of course you didn't," Doña Laura soothed. "Sometimes the shells that make us grownups come apart. Maker needs a little time to put his back together."

Biting her lip, Libertad took the money and hurried away. Doña Laura waited while Maker struggled with his emotions. Finally, red-eyed and embarrassed, the old bricoleur snuffled. His host waited until he looked up.

"The girl is only nine," Doña Laura observed. "It was not her charm that overthrew you."

"No," he agreed, "Your granddaughter–"

"Second cousin of my great grandson's wife," she corrected.

"Second cou–"

Maker cut himself off.

Doña Laura shrugged.

"We are both orphans. We take care of each other. But it's not about the girl."

She leaned her forearms onto her knees.

"What has happened?"

It took no more than that to open the gates. Maker told her. The story came out as a jumble, pride in his bird inextricable from shame and outrage at the abuse of Carlotta.

Doña Laura listened until he was done.

"I didn't call the police," he admitted, but she held up a hand to forestall him.

"*Entiendo,*" she said. "I understand. The police would not protect you."

Maker nodded. Doña Laura reached to pat his knee.

"Against the animal, I have no answers, but for your magic bird, maybe something."

She dragged a box from under her table and pushed it toward him.

Maker opened the flaps and removed a layer of packing. Inside nested an antique mantle clock, a small monument in brass and mahogany. He lifted it onto his lap.

"There's no key to wind it," Doña Laura told him, "But I never imagined that would trouble you."

"Where did you find this?"

Maker turned the clock to view all angles.

The glass over the face was broken out. Metal pieces clinked inside. Between the numeral 2 and the center, his little finger fit snugly into a black rimed hole aligned with an impact pimple on the steel back.

"Estate sale," she told him. "Saw it and thought of you."

Maker placed the clock on Doña Laura's table and drew his tool wallet from a pocket. With a screwdriver first and then a pick, he pried open the back. Broken metal clattered free, bounced off the case and dropped to the floor. He turned the clock face down.

Doña Laura pointed to the fragment, saying, "I did my best to make sure all the pieces were still inside. I remember you said it's important to get as much as possible."

He glanced in the direction she indicated, nodding thanks without taking his attention from the clock. Several gears and as many bearings had been destroyed, as had the mainspring, but a large part of the mechanism was intact.

"It's from that commissioner. The murder-suicide?"

Doña Laura carefully lowered herself to retrieve the fragment from the floor.

Maker seemed not to listen. She went on.

"The guy that shot his wife? As I heard it, she turned as he fired. The bullet went lung, heart, lung without touching bone. The clock caught the round, her dying breath and her life's blood."

She held up the metal shard.

"If it's all the same to you, I'll keep this one little piece. I'm not going to say there is power in such things, but I've lived a long time with my eyes open, and I'm not going to say there isn't, either."

With his pick, Maker advanced a gear, watching the mechanism closely. The second hand fell loose, but the minute hand clicked forward. He saw no apparent damage to the drive for the hour hand, nor to the subassemblies for day and date.

Doña Laura clutched the table with one hand when she rose. The other disappeared into her pocket with the sliver of metal.

Coughing to clear her throat, she spat into a wastebasket, and finished, "After the *pendejo* shot her, he stuck the gun under his chin and blew the top of his skull into the ceiling."

Maker turned the clock face up and gave it a shake. A few more fragments fell out. He swept these into a pile on the table.

"*Señora,*" he nodded to his friend, "You tell the most uplifting stories."

The old vendor chuckled.

"Happy to spread the love, Maker!"

Turning serious, she declared, "Forty bucks, two dozen brass flowers, and you fix the mangle on my granddaughter's washer."

"Dreamer!" Maker retorted. "Ten in scrip and six flowers. The mangle is separate. I'll do it for fifty grams of coffee. Real coffee. Whole beans."

"You're a thief at heart," Doña Laura countered. "I have always said so. Twenty-five in scrip, a dozen flowers, and thirty grams of coffee."

"Eighteen, with a coffee right now, separate from the mangle."

Doña Laura de las Casas grinned. She held out her hand as Libertad approached with a canister, then turned to fire her stove.

"Done," she agreed, sparking the striker.

Tugging his cart across the threshold, Maker entered the well of his building. He started toward the stairs, but looked up and stopped. Excitement over the clock had overthrown him. He was home early. Bear leaned on the rail above, watching.

"What you got, old man? Need a hand?"

The sound of that voice came down on Maker with weight he did not think he could bear. He sagged. His joints cracked audibly. Ache raced up the back of his skull.

He was afraid.

The silence grew.

"I'm fi-fine, thank you," he stammered.

Bear came down anyway.

"Take it while you can get it, old man. Otherwise," Bear's eyebrows bobbed archly, "It might take you."

Grabbing the cart, he lifted with a grunt.

"Damn!" he exclaimed. "What do you have in here? This weighs a ton."

Maker said nothing.

Outside the door, Bear hugged the cart to his chest instead of setting it down while Maker sorted keys. Pushing past the old man, he placed it crossways, obstructing the entry. Bear surveyed the room.

"So this is the crap that makes the racket."

He wandered to a bench and stood looking at the objects covering it.

"These are things I have made," Maker replied. "Some of them have voices."

Bear closed his hand around a ballerina, testing its sturdiness with his thumb. The fabric of its costume tore away from the breast, revealing a carefully sculpted nipple.

Bear snorted.

"A pervert, huh? I like that."

He ripped away the dancer's clothing.

Prodding at the seams where legs and torso joined, he tsked.

"You got the pussy wrong."

Waving the dancer at Maker, he scoffed, "No wonder you listen at keyholes. You don't even know the shape of a honey box."

Cowed at first, Maker grew hot at the vandalism.

"Getting the movement right mattered. Not the anatomy."

Bear turned, letting the dancer's tutu fall to the floor. He dropped the figure on the bench. With two steps, he crossed the space between them and jabbed a finger at the old man.

"The rest of the furniture is nice, but when it comes to a Betty, her box is the only thing that matters. You'd know that if you spent more time wetting your presto and less time listening to what you think you hear."

Laughing at his own wit, Bear shoved past and went out.

Maker slammed the door and shoved the cart aside with his hip. He went to the bird and cranked with rough fury. The song burst out, ragged and clamorous.

From the next apartment came, "Damn! Not that effing tinkle!"

That was enough. Snatching his hand from the crank, Maker retrieved the clock. Within minutes he had the works pulled from the body and begun disassembly. Damaged parts he placed by the scanner; intact parts, he laid out by the bird.

Soon, he was lost in the process. Working out recombinations, scanning, modifying or reinventing, he saw where he wanted gears to go, and made necessary pieces on the fly. Curves flowed past his inner eye. From the shapes, he spoke aloud sums and products like reading music from a staff.

The scanner hummed, capturing shattered pieces. The printer buzzed as it built replacements. Maker's hands danced over the screen of his antique tablet, or flipped a jeweler's loupe over his eye as he used forceps, picks and tiny screwdrivers to build a new version of the clockwork inside the bird.

The superseded crank went carefully into a box in the storeroom.

He retained as much of the original clock as possible. Doña Laura's account hung close. Discarding without need would dishonor the murdered woman. Where no existing part or broken piece would work, he fabricated anew. Whatever he could make serve, he did.

Finished at last, the bricoleur stood back to contemplate what he had wrought. His hands twitched, but he could not bring himself immediately to wind the spring and release the catch.

Tracing the drive visually, he had no doubt it would work. It was too beautiful, too balanced not to work.

Roughly half the assembly was original clock, including seven of the jewel bearings. The substitutes for those lost were exact copies down to crystalline structure, but he considered the seven originals the only real jewels in the mechanism. Seven tiny bearings from a clock that had caught a dying breath, a life's blood and a killing shot.

The sense of Doña Laura's statement finally got through to him.

"I'm not going to say there is power in such things…and I'm not going to say there isn't, either."

He knew without question that the bird

would sing. What he did not know was how he would react when the bird sang and he had nothing to do but listen.

Minutes lapsed. He began to feel foolish.

At last, he wound the spring, released the catch, and stopped as though seized.

Melody belled into the room. The shifts of scale and cylinder were seamless. Resonant notes streamed. Between this and the hand-cranked bird was a vastness he could not have imagined.

Maker sank to his knees.

When the evening sun sank enough to leave the room in twilight, he opened his eyes. The bird was silent. Maker sat cross-legged on the floor, a position he had not attempted in recent memory.

Hours had passed since the encounter with Bear. Rising, he stretched, surprised that he did so with no creaking. A fleeting thought of supper escaped his interest.

The cart still sat where Bear had placed it. Maker had taken nothing from it except the clock. He moved to stow the rest, whistling softly, not realizing that he echoed the bird.

At the first gunshot, Maker rolled from the recliner to the floor. Instincts from another era, another name, another life, reacted even before he woke, much less wondered what had happened. The next two shots came rapidly, one after another, originating from the landing outside his apartment.

A voice he recognized as Bear's friend Rufer shouted, "Crap!"

Another person, unknown, guffawed.

A fourth shot was followed by Bear's announcement, "Look and learn, morons."

Rufer, sounding sour, advised, "We better get inside. I bet the cops are already on the way."

Maker lay on the floor as Bear led his guests into his apartment. Their laughter and bragging came through the wall. So did Bear's explanation for Carlotta's absence.

"She took off a few days ago after Rufer and me popped her threesome cherry."

"That was cool as hell," chimed Rufer.

"It was," Bear agreed, "But she was pissed and took off. Her dog's still here, so I'm not worried. Anyway, all you guys get in the meantime is beer and donuts."

"Beer and donuts, haha!" Rufer laughed. "Hey! We could have fun with her dog."

"What do you mean?" Bear snapped. "You want to hurt a dumb animal? Jesus, Rufer! That's repulsive!"

It took a second for Maker to realize the next sound was Rufer sputtering.

"Chill out, Bear," the third man said. "I don't think he was serious."

"Causing pain to something that can't understand the reason?" Bear shouted. "That's totally serious! Nobody touches that dog! Rufer?"

When his friend did not respond, Bear yelled, "Quit waving your hands and answer me! What do you have to say, Rufer?"

"Bear, I'm sorry."

Rufer's voice shook.

"It was a joke. I didn't mean anything."

Though Maker strained to hear, there was a long pause before any reaction came. He imagined his neighbor's stony cold glare.

"All right, then," Bear conceded at last.

The third man changed the subject.

"So that domestic call on your record was no problem?"

Bear laughed, his dominance reaffirmed. "Didn't even look at it."

"I'm gonna get one!" Rufer declared.

Maker went into his back room, and closed the door.

The voices of the men in the next apartment were muffled but reached him. He climbed atop the boxes stacked in the closet, pulled shut the sliding panels, and clutched his arms over his ears.

When he started out to go to the market, Maker discovered police and private security working in front of the building across the street. He paused on the landing, looking at the scene framed by the courtyard entrance. The door of the other apartment opened a few inches. Bear stood inside, staring, out of sight from all but his neighbor.

Directly below a voice said, "Thank you for your time."

A moment later an officer started up the stairs. Bear's eyes narrowed. He shook a finger at the old man, stepped back and closed his door.

Spying Maker, the officer called as she reached the landing, "Sir, may I ask you a few questions?"

His voice cracked when he answered.

"Of course. What's going on?"

"Someone shot up downspouts on the building across the way. A slug penetrated the wall and destroyed property inside an apartment. We're also trying to determine if this incident is connected to a projectile that struck a pedestrian a couple blocks from here. Have you been home all morning?"

"Oh! Oh! Struck! You mean…?"

"She'll recover," the officer assured him. "Have you been home all morning?"

"Yes, ma'am. I heard the shots. I mean, I guess they were shots. They were more like cracks than bangs. That's what woke me."

The officer adjusted her voice recorder. "Cracks?"

"Right. Cracks. Crack, crack! Like when a really big tree branch breaks."

"I understand. That's useful. When was this?"

"An hour ago, maybe. I tried to go back to sleep, but that didn't happen. I finally gave up and got up."

The officer waited to see if he would volunteer more.

When he did not, she asked, "Is there anything else you can tell me?"

Though he looked away, she caught his distress. She waited.

"I heard voices," he finally admitted. "But I was afraid to look."

She cocked her head.

"I have to live here," he stated flatly.

She said nothing.

Maker explained testily, "All kinds come and go here. Some are not forgiving. Some of them have memories."

The officer sighed, and shook her head.

"What about you, sir?" she resumed. "Do you own a gun?"

Maker thought for a second, then nodded. Turning back toward his door he motioned for her to follow. The officer stepped inside the apartment, and stopped. Her head swept right and left trying to take in the sea of shapes.

"This is amazing!" she exclaimed. "What is this stuff?"

Maker went to a bench and started moving flowers off a wooden box. It was obviously a purpose-made case.

"This is my work," he told her. "This is what I do."

Lifting the box, he turned and held it out.

"I know who you are," the officer declared, taking it from him. "I've heard about you."

Inside the case lay a long-barreled, single-shot pistol of brass, silver and bone. Three cartridges sat snug in individual slots aligned below the barrel. The gun required two hands to load and two to cock. Two of the bullets were plain, but the third was inscribed with tiny symbols.

"What?" she asked, lifting the gun from its bed. "I've never seen anything like this."

Hefting it, she sighted along the barrel.

"I can't even tell what caliber it is. Where did you get it?"

She looked up.
"Wait! Did you *make* this?"
He nodded. The officer whistled.
"The ammo, too?"
He nodded, flushing.
"Why only three?"
He blinked, surprised by the question.
"Two are for testing," he told her. "If it should ever come to a test."
She sniffed the barrel.
"You made this but you never fired it?"
She looked incredulous. Maker shrugged.
"It's an instrument, not a weapon."
He smiled.
"I have no plans to pack it on the street."
The explanation obviously bothered her. Perplexity made her awkward, juggling the case in one hand and pistol in the other.
Slipping the box into the crook of her arm, she remarked, almost casually, "But if two are for testing, that leaves just one shot."
"If the tests are successful," he explained, "One is all I'll ever need."
Troubled by his answer, the officer started to respond, but stopped herself.
Returning the gun to its case, she handed it back and thanked him. He followed her to the door as she went out. Crossing to the other apartment, she knocked and waited,

knocked again and waited. Then, with a casual salute to Maker, she turned and left. He stood in his doorway, watching her climb the steps.

When her knock sounded on the floor above, the door across the landing opened slightly. Bear looked out from the shadows.

He was mounting the stairs when he heard the blow land.

"She came back!" Maker thought, despairing. "Why did she come back?"

The rhythmic hitting began as he locked himself inside. Fist struck flesh with nauseating regularity: first a smack, then the thump of a body into wall or furniture. Maker was winding the bird when he heard ceramic shatter.

Bear shouted, "You bitch!"

Then silence.

Then Carlotta's voice, shrill with panic.

"You're pointing a gun at me, Bear? Really? Really?"

Maker started the bird. He jerked the lever to open the resonator wide. The clockwork with seven original jewels drove cylinder spines into ancient scales. Music boomed from the pedestal.

Bobbing and turning, the bird fluttered its wings. Its beak opened and closed.

"That effing old man!" Bear roared. "Don't move!"

The door of the neighbors' apartment slammed wide. The knob punched through drywall with an unmistakable thump.

Bear pounded on Maker's door. When it did not instantly open, he splintered it with his shoulder. The music struck as he realized Carlotta and her dog were rushing the stairs.

For the first time, Bear heard the bird unmuted by a wall. Jolted beneath his rage, he staggered.

Without turning, Carlotta stopped cold in her flight.

The song of the bird stabbed into Bear. Erupting from nowhere, anguish drove his heart so hard that he grabbed at his chest.

He swung the pistol wildly, trying all at once to cow Maker, Carlotta, and the ache, the inexplicable ache, exploding in his core.

By the time Bear shot, Maker had ceased distinguishing the finger on the trigger from the woman on the stair, the hulk at his door, or his own weary bones. Purged of remorse, the old man lofted away from threat or fear.

In the ordinary world, a body fell and bled out. Two others froze, a death split three ways.

The bird wound down with its spring, sounded a final note and went still. It sat long moments before, through the open door, a siren keened in the distance.

THE END

Acknowledgments

For abiding friendship to these fictions, the author thanks: Paul E. Cooley, Jim Eidson, Thomas Fang, Chuck Gatlin and William Jackson, David Gray, Mary Jo Jirik-Wong, Bill Luthans, Kenneth Kidder, Mark Lewis, Carla Maywald, Amanda McMullen, Thomas O'Hara , James Rossignol, Nancy Salay, Mary Saunders, Paula Torres, Tom Wheeler

Also by Robert Stikmanz:

Rose Moon & Death on the Toilet
ISBN 9780983813743

Prelude to a Change of Mind, the Author's
Edition
ISBN 9780983813798

Dvarsh, An Introduction
ISBN 9780983813767

Dvarsh Workbook: Beginning Exercises for
the Extraordinary Student
ISBN 9780983813774

Nod's Way, the Author's Edition
ISBN 9781732118737

The Song of Worlds (Dzadefve Oa Charls'm)
ISBN 9781732118706

www.ingramcontent.com/pod-product-compliance
Lightning Source LLC
Chambersburg PA
CBHW031753200726
48289CB00013B/928